about the author

Gary Percesepe is Associate Editor at *New World Writing* (formerly *Mississippi Review*) and a Contributor at *The Nervous Breakdown*. Author of four books in philosophy, Percesepe's poetry, fiction, essays, and interviews have appeared in *Story Quarterly*, *N + 1*, *Salon*, *Mississippi Review*, *The Millions*, *Brevity*, *PANK*, *Wigleaf*, *Metazen*, *The Brooklyner*, and other places.

His collection of short stories, *Why I Did the Grocery Girl*, is forthcoming from Aqueous Books.

Percesepe has taught at Saint Louis University, Wittenberg University, and University of Dayton.

praise for *itch*

Gary Percesepe writes beautiful, vivid stories with the intensity and brevity of a man on the run. His fiction lights up the page with incredible bursts of poetry, passion, and pain channeled through characters whose names we rarely catch. In just a few short pages, Percesepe captures entire worlds of emotion – all of it so true and real, it's impossible to look away.

Jessica Anya Blau, author of *The Wonder Bread Summer*

itch is a shrewd, swift–moving collection about urges, obsessions, and the energy of desire. Gary Percesepe's stories work together to expose and examine a curious cycle – the way our reality drives our fantasies and our fantasies influence our reality.

Jen Knox, author of *Don't Tease the Elephants*

Where is it that our days go? Into the big dark American night, and they take with them their secrets. Gary Percesepe's stories have made the return trip: they pulse, they tremble and radiate with a life we might have thought we had lost. Keep *Itch* close. Have it near for your quiet hours, your spells of wayward dreamtime.

Scott Garson, author of *Is That You, John Wayne?*

These rapid and arresting short stories will keep you on your toes. Percesepe is a master of sharp turns, and, oh, how greatly I admire the stuff he notices, all of life's "brilliant surprises," and his concern with how people who bust up stay apart, because what can we do with the delayed understanding that happens after the leaving? This collection is a tender rush.

Pia Ehrhardt, author of *Famous Fathers & Other Stories.*

An absolutely entrancing collection. These are the stories of women and girls remembered, longed for, and lost. The girlfriends and wives and lovers and crushes and the singular gestures that crack open the hearts of men. This collection unearths what lies just beneath the surface, what cannot be ignored. The itch that demands your attention. When Percesepe opens with: "A woman I knew died decades before her burial," well, you pull up a chair, knowing you are in the hands of a master storyteller. That he does what he does in the space of a page or two and with such precision and grace is its own small miracle.

Kathy Fish, author of *Together We Can Bury It* and *Wild Life*

There are no apologies in the aptly titled *itch*, but primal desire ... Gary Percesepe is a courageous writer willing to explore what terrifies and obsesses us ...

Kimberlee Smith

Gary Percesepe's literary and film criticism is acute, his fiction startling, evocative, funny, and richly felt, and his poetry meditative and piercing. His political essays are compelling and right—minded, hard by truth to power, and always deserving. I cannot recommend his work highly enough. Everything he writes challenges us in the best possible way.

Frederick Barthelme

Gary Percesepe drops you into an ambiguous world and pulls you back again, still reeling. He does it so deftly, you don't even realize you're bleeding until it's over.

Heather Cox, author of *California King*

itch is a book of love and heartbreak. Its characters move through the world with passion. Each line is filled with grace and longing: tender and yet bold. Refreshingly told, Gary Percesepe has written a book of gold and magic.

Kim Chinquee, author of *Pretty* and *Oh Baby: Flash Fictions and Prose Poetry*

also by Gary Percesepe

fiction

Why I Did the Grocery Girl
forthcoming

What May Have Been:
Letters of Jackson Pollock & Dori G
with Susan Tepper

poetry

falling and other poems

philosophy

Ethics: Personal and Social Responsibility in a Diverse World

Free Spirits: Feminist Philosophers on Culture
with Kate Mehuron

Philosophy: An Introduction to the Labor of Reason

Future(s) of Philosophy:
The Marginal Thinking of Jacques Derrida

itch

itch

Gary Percesepe

a Pure Slush book

Pure
Slush

itch published by Pure Slush, November 2013.

All stories copyright © Gary Percesepe

Front cover design copyright © Pier Rodelon

Author photograph copyright © Jeff Smith

ISBN: 978−1−925101−21−8

You can find *Pure Slush* at http://pureslush.webs.com

Copies of all *Pure Slush* publications can be bought
at http://pureslush.webs.com/store.htm

All queries re *Pure Slush* can be made
via email to edpureslush@live.com.au

for Nichole

Contents

Beautiful Girls

I was trying to figure what it was about women's feet when a cop stopped me. He approached my car, lumbering. I fingered my Native shades. He said remove your eyewear. I said OK. He said you from around here? I said, well, I guess.

He studied me and went back to his car with my license. Wait right there, he said. Here? I said.

I voicemailed over to my outgoing message, to see what I sounded like when I was sober.

The cop came back and said did I know I was doing 85? I couldn't feature that, so I said so. It was a time for honesty.

I was thinking about women's feet, I said. What is it about them?

The cop had a badge that said Danny. It looked like Dandy.

In *Vogue* the woman's feet are strapped and loaded. The colors make me weep. Do they put makeup on feet? I see a heel on a cool blonde I wanna cry. I told this to Danny.

My wife has corns, he said. She makes me rub them. I have this special rub I do only for her. He shakes his head. God damn. When we first married I would give her foot massages. You see what I'm saying? He shakes again, hands me the ticket. His hat is off and his head is pattern bald. He replaces the hat and shakes my hand. Thank you, I say.

She can't wear heels, now, Danny says. Sensibles only. She goes around everywhere in flats or flip flops. She has the veins. Three kids. Christ, it's probably my fault.

I nod, but am afraid to use the voice. He's on to something.

Michelle Pfeiffer, Danny says. You remember? That mob movie? She gets a foot rub?

I try my voice. Uma Thurman, I say. The great debate with John Travolta and Samuel L. Jackson about did she or didn't she get a foot massage from thus and so. That didn't sound right. I waited.

Now Uma, Danny says, she has the flat feet. Funny toes. I dunno about her.

Beautiful Girls, I say. You ever see that movie?

Nope. Danny checks his watch.

I pocket my ticket. I smile and replace the Natives. Then I salute. That doesn't seem right, so I slurve my hand over to part my hair.

But Uma, Danny says. She was amazing in *Kill Bill*. Real scary. I like that.

Beautiful Girls, I say. She is the perfect girl from Chicago. In this movie, see? She says to the guys, I'm looking for a man who can say to me at the end of the day just four words. Good night sweet girl. Just that.

Just like that.

Like that.

Women's feet, I say.

It's the arch, Danny says. She hangs her foot by your mouth. Beyond the reach of tragedy. Speed dial the pope. Sweet Jesus.

We nod in agreement.

Gail

In seventh grade Gail Robasco was the girl we all wanted. She was what our mothers called "well–developed", which to us meant that she had big tits. She also had long brown hair and huge brown eyes which even too much blue eye shadow couldn't ruin. Her skin was creamy white, as though she never saw the sun, and her skinny legs were often encased in black fish–net stockings, the rage in 1967. But I liked her voice, which was uncertain, like she was afraid to let the words get too far away from her, and tiny for such a big girl. Talking to Gail was like an invitation to get closer to those tits.

She liked me, I thought. She liked to flirt, especially in Mr. Cyr's history class, where I always got into trouble. I made her laugh. One day Cyr caught us passing notes. "Mr. Thomas, come forward," he said in his theatrical baritone. Everything with him was such an event. I reminded myself as I walked up to the front of the class that this man was the eighth grade bowling coach, for Christ's sake, that I couldn't let him break my dignity. He grabbed my shoulders, squared me up, then turned me around and kicked me in the ass. I didn't make a sound. After, when I turned around to look at Gail she gave me this look that I wanted to save forever.

One day at Bobby's house we practiced what we would do when we finally got Gail alone, how we aimed to kiss her and feel her up. We made up a clumsy code of words and moves that we thought might work, stuff I'd heard guys talk about in metal shop class. We had signals for when to French kiss, when to grope her tits, when to take the beaver shot. I watched Bobby squirm around on the couch, grinding his hips and kissing the pillow, and I called out the code words at what I thought were the right moments. Later, he did the same for me. We were men.

The next week she got kidnapped and raped by a man in his thirties. When they caught him they put his picture in the paper so we could all look. There was a story under the picture, I remember, though I noticed they left out the rape part. I studied the words, the peculiar black and white pattern they formed on that awful page, the way they referred somehow to Gail: minor, undisclosed location, allegedly, protect. When Gail came back to class all she got from us was silence. She limped, and every time our eyes met I would look away, or at the hospital gauze on her white thigh that kept slipping down her leg as Mr. Cyr talked. The stockings were gone.

It's funny: I don't remember seeing her again after that, not in high school, not anywhere, though I'm sure I must have. We lived in a small town. How could I have missed her?

I'm older now. I have two sons of my own. I've never told them about Gail. What would I say? *When I was your age I knew this kid, a classmate. I was really hot for her, you know? We never did anything about it, though. We were kids. Then one day, she was gone. Just like that. I don't know what happened to her. I can't find any of my high school notebooks, or my notes from college, even. Yearbooks, graduation cap, tassel, gone, all of it. At the time you thought it was important. You thought it would all be there for you, somehow. Life is like that. Things change. You don't know how or why but they do. You just look up one day and everything is gone. Cells of your skin die every minute, second by second, from the time you are born, brain cells decay, you lose what you most wanted to save, and the ghosts carry the rest away. Trust me on this.*

Now, I sit at home late at night and try to imagine what she looked like. I sit at this keyboard and try to remember her into existence. I tap her back into my life lovingly, one keystroke at a time. Gail is at our twentieth year high school reunion, drinking by herself at a corner table, and her voice hasn't changed. I still have to lean into her to listen.

Christmas

My first girlfriend had blue Christmas lights strung on trees in front of her stone house. My family had all gone to bed. When midnight came, it was snowing. The streets were silent as I drove. Snow filled the lumberyards of Peekskill along the Hudson River. I'd gotten a wool sweater, some gloves, a navy blazer with gold buttons, gray pants. A wet kiss from my father, his holiday tears. She was in her wooden bed, high on the second floor, beneath the dormer. I parked in her driveway, cut the engine, listened to it tick. Her house was filled with brilliant surprises, narrow white feet and her girlish sleep. It'd be years before I returned. She'd be a teacher, I'd be married, my grandfather dead, my grandmother still in the kitchen in her worn housedress. The lumberyards along the river would be empty. She'd hold me all through the night. We'd try to sort the past, but everything had fled, her innocence, small chin, the thinness of her wrists. She'd lay beside me on the couch in her terrible insignificance, the life we never lived dissolved to tears. But that Christmas in her driveway snowflakes like diamonds stuck to the curved windshield of my father's Ford. I waited for the sun to rise, like a story.

Itch

On the day he learns of his wife's affair Tom Friendly watches
the girl drummer of White Stripes wail away at it somewhere in
Canada. The girl is good, her long dark hair matted against her
pale skin as she feverishly bounces up and down on her seat and
keeps the beat and joins her brother in the vocals at the chorus.
He hadn't known the two were related, and while he thinks it
kind of creepy, the way they look at each other on stage, he had
just been admiring her pale white legs and strappy shoes walking
the tarmac in the Yukon. Tom nods on the phone, even though
Elise, who is 1,000 miles away in Chicago, cannot see his nods.
She explains how sorry she is and Tom elects generosity,
accepting her apology but not requesting details even when
proffered. They have been separated for three months and Tom
has himself proposed an affair with a young woman he has
recently met in Boston on a book tour.

Tom replaces the phone in its cradle, grabs his car keys, and
goes to the Rite Aide. For two days he has been itching without
relief. It is late August and his skin is dried out from too many
days lazing at the pool, exhausted from his book tour. He asks a
clerk where to find the health and beauty products and is
directed to two long aisles cluttered with products whose names
he does not recognize.

He hadn't expected to meet anyone so soon, or maybe ever.
But Anastasia had looked up at him from the first row of the
auditorium where he had been giving a reading and it was not
what she said — she hadn't said a word, too shy to ask a question
in the exchange afterwards — but just the way she had allowed

others to crowd forward in front of her, knock–kneed in her clumsy Doc Martens, the way she looked up at him and then stepped aside. She'd buzzed off her hair, a beautiful girl tired of false attention, and placed herself in the background, but Tom saw and understood her as a woman willing to do what was necessary to start again. Tom knew that Elise had been having the affair but kept his mouth shut, knowing she would tell him when she was ready. And now he has nothing to say. He can't tell her about Anastasia because nothing had happened. Just that graceful stepping aside, the taking of an auditorium seat while she waited for him, a cup of coffee afterwards, and a few hundred emails between distant cities.

Tom Friendly walks slowly down the aisle lifting products from the shelves, struggling to read the small print on bath oils, beads, salts, scented body wash with aloe, topical creams, cocoa butter. He doesn't know what he needs and feels too foolish to ask for help. His skin appears normal but feels harsh and irritated. The itch travels, reconstituting in a different place on his body each time he scratches. He gathers one item from every shelf and leaves with $82.89 of merchandise. The pretty redhead who takes his money – he has only a hundred dollar bill – makes change and attempts a joke about self–medicating, but Tom is itching so badly he only smiles grimly, nods at the girl, and speeds home.

He strips off his clothes and draws a bath, dumping in a $20 package of salts from the Dead Sea and lavender bath oil. While the water is running, Tom adjusts the small TV mounted on the bathroom wall until he finds the station with the boy and girl band. The documentary is still on the air. Sister and brother are visiting with the Inuit people of a small village in Canada. Then they are giving a concert, and now the girl is singing, off key and earnest, and her skin so white and plain, and he thinks of Anastasia feeding her child eggs at the breakfast table, her husband rushing out the door to work and it cracks open his heart.

Tom dabs his eyes and reaches behind in a futile effort to scratch his sore back, then grinds his shoulder blades up against the doorpost for relief. He steps into the bath. Leaning back in the tub, he stretches out until his head rests on the shelf behind him, and his toes reach up into the cascading hot water. Brother and sister sing, "Jolene, Jolene, please don't take him," and later, the girl is speaking in a subdued tone, embarrassed by the two cameras capturing her every word and gesture in a botched impromptu interview, and her cloying brother – is he really her brother or is this too an act? – teasing her for her shyness and speaking over her.

Tom opens a jar of coffee–colored cream. The cocoa butter smells sweet and inviting. He slides his fingers deep into the cool cream and lavishes it up and down his arms, his chest, his inner thighs and calves. The jar holds the trace of his fingers in four parallel tracks matching the scratches he has placed on his body with nervous nails. He pulls out the plug and feels his cracked skin relax, tired pores open. Gravity sucks away the gray used water. He watches the girl twirl her sticks and pound her drums.

Go

She left with the check. Ford watched her go. With feline grace she slunk around the corner to the cash register of the Waffle House, where she looked back at him over her high shoulder.

She was wearing the dress Ford had bought for her the night before (U.S. size 0, Italian size 36, UK size 4). It was a Betsey Johnson little black dress, with Betsey's signature "I can't help myself" splash of color, lavender rose petals – a flare dress with lace twenty inches from the waist. Her bare legs were tan and fit. With her small bust and toned arms, she looked built for speed, even at 7 am, after a night of dancing.

She was comically overdressed for the Waffle House and she was enjoying it. She twirled in place while three women groggily paid their bill, and the man in front of her, a lucky gray head, the wife sleeping at home or dead, smiled at her. She returned the smile and shook his hand. He beamed from ear to ear. She wore a pair of Jimmy Choo silk satin peep toe shoes with jewelled buckles that Ford had also bought, along with a black Kate Spade clutch purse. She'd shucked the $900 shoes off to dance barefoot through the night. The shoes landed against the dirty wall of the Nashville night spot, where a waiter retrieved them and placed them on her chair. The soles of her feet (size six) were smooth and dirty.

Ford watched from the table where they had shared breakfast. A waitress bussed their plates and silverware. Corrine – was that her name? – had picked at her pancake, stabbing and swimming pieces around in a sea of maple syrup, then banking them into uneaten mounds at the edge of the plate. He guessed her to be 105 pounds, 108 at the outside (7 stone, 8 lbs). Within range. He had stopped at Bergdorf Goodman, spotted her in Gloves, given her his card, and had her on a plane by noon. She wanted to tell her mother. Ford had agreed to stop. He frequently did. The mother lived on the other side of the interstate. She was going home.

Ford watched her pay the bill. He had the chauffeur on the phone. The car was brought around. She ducked into the Ladies room. Ford stepped outside. He lit a cigarette, took a drag, and stubbed it out against the peeling paint of the diner. Fierce sunlight glinted off his sunglasses. He threw his Armani jacket into the limo, slammed the door shut. The chauffer rolled down his window. Bending at the waist, Ford leaned in the window. He peeled off ten hundred dollar bills from his clip and handed them to the chauffer. He made his instructions plain.

He walked east. Another plane awaited. Overnight to many distant cities.

Snowed In

Atlantic City, January 4. The children are with her mother in Trenton. On their tenth anniversary, rain lashes the windows, turns to snow, then back to rain. It is two o'clock in the morning. Doctors from the convention stumble into elevators. One tries their door with a keycard, curses his mistake, shuffles off down the hall.

Our lives were built on false information, Tyrone tells Anna, but that doesn't mean tonight can't be different?

They have argued. They are the couple who bicker at weddings.

Outside, rain sifts through parking lot trees. Smashed perfection, Anna says. Though we started well. Our first year we didn't ever fight.

He considers this. Maybe we should have fought, he says. His voice bleeds into the upper register. People fight when they have complete relationships. You know? Not based on fantasy.

I'm tired of fighting, she says. You're one to talk, about fantasies.

I gave her up, Tyrone pleads.

You said that, Anna says.

But it's true. I only held her once and it probably doesn't count. I never kissed her. Didn't even try. We were walking to the 14th Street station after dinner and I grabbed her waist and pulled her to my side in a guy half hug, OK? And she kind of hung there at my hip, for two beats. Then we released and we were at the station and I tried to convince her but she said she couldn't, ever. She walked down the stairs and I called her name and she turned back around and looked but I couldn't, either.

Is this supposed to make me feel better?

Tyrone sighs, and walks to the window. It has turned to snow, again. They are calling for a blizzard to hit. If it does they will be snowed in. They have two more nights at the conference. He looks over his shoulder and shudders. Wind escapes the night and passes through the double—paned hotel window. He starts to draw the curtains, then reconsiders at the sight of the swollen blizzard moon. It is a furious season. Already, a continent away in Malibu, red—tiled mansions slide toward the sea, carried by rivers of mud. Her body is tiny in the ridiculously big bed. She looks like a small enemy.

I don't know what it is supposed to make you feel. But it's the truth.

The truth, she snorts. Yes. Well.

She turns her back to him but continues to speak.

There are always more worlds to travel. And this is not about your silly girl. But when it becomes time to go neither of us will leave before the other. And that's because of the first year.

Tyrone lies beside her in bed reading Tolstoy, in trouble again with the church despite being dead one hundred years. Anna's back curves like the half moon of winter. Tyrone watches with stupid tears as she places her clear fingernails lightly beneath his ache as if she were touching an altar of driftwood.

Her mouth opens to him, their love a pier extending far out into the swollen river.

Last Stop

The train started at West 4th Street and sped downtown under
rivers and snow soiled and black from the exhausted city till it
came to the last stop at Rockaway Beach, where it rose above
ground, passing over white–topped buses and immigrant
mothers who pushed strollers through the clogged streets below,
unaware that above them, a man studied the way that they
moved. Mitch Stern had started the day in Poughkeepsie. After
quarrelling with his wife about the terms of their divorce he had
slammed the front door and walked to the train station. He
found himself in Grand Central Terminal, where he bought a
black and white cookie and studied the roiled stock market
report on the broadsheet of the *Wall Street Journal*, though he
no longer had any stock. We loved each other once, he had said,
slamming the door behind him. Before, Miranda looked at him,
pitiless. She'd nicked her finger on the serrated edge of a can
throwing out the trash, and sucked a bloodied finger. She ran the
blood–fingered hand through her hair, then stopped and placed
her hands on her hips, waiting. The door slam followed. But
then, coatless in the snow, walking, Mitch had an image of the
way all things end at the shore, there at the end of the world,
and he rode the train until he saw the Atlantic Ocean crash
lonely onto an empty winter beach. He got off the train and
walked toward the water. On the horizon wind pushed up
whitecaps. Gulls glided above the cold gray currents.

With Mary

Downstairs was crowded and too many voices were speaking at once. I lost sight of Mary. Some people huddled in a corner by the stage. The microphone was still on the stage but I did not know where Mary had gone. A couple looked at me as though I should know them.

A woman came up and threw her arms around me. She thanked me. Her voice was hoarse and she coughed into her starfish hand. She apologized for coughing but her perfume was lovely. It hung there between us. I wondered where Mary had gone. The couple by the stage continued to look.

I left the room with my bag under my arm. Mary was at the bar in the next room. She came up to me and took my arm. A photographer wanted to take our picture. Mary sent him away after one flash. My eyes stung. I wondered where our picture would appear.

A waiter went for a taxi. Outside it was hot and bright from the camera lights. They were filming the outside of the bar. Equipment and cars filled the street. The street was shaped like a little square. A fountain had appeared in the square and water tumbled. There were trees and grass and on the grass taxis were parked. One drove toward us and the waiter opened the door. Mary got in. I tipped the waiter and got into the taxi beside Mary.

I told the driver where to drive and he shot out of there. Ruts formed in the grass as he accelerated. We entered a long tunnel. I told Mary what she had said to me the last time I saw her. That I made her laugh. She frowned and said, did I say that? She smiled then and I saw her white teeth.

The tunnel was dark. Mary moved close to me. We sat close to one another without speaking. I put my arm around her and tried to see where we were headed. At the end of the tunnel was a long hill and we climbed the hill in second gear. Outside the houses were white stucco lit by floodlight.

We crossed a bridge. The water was black beneath us. I told the driver to stop. I got out of the car. I took Mary's hand and she got out. I told the driver to wait. With Mary, I stood on the bridge and watched the black water move. A bat flew into the open window of the taxi and the driver yelled and the bat flew out. We watched the bat fly off into the night. I asked Mary if she felt alright and she said she felt fine. It was hot and dark. A light flashed on in a house across the river and then it flashed out.

Girl, Interrupted

When his wife asked him for a divorce M drove down the New York State Thruway into Manhattan and checked into the Pierre Hotel.

Catherine hadn't been specific; it had been understood for some time that things were not working. M pouted, pleaded, tried to be charming, threw a fit, attempted to argue her out of it, and finally resorted to negotiating, but nothing worked. Catherine was firm. "Look, let's just forget it," she'd said.

M chose New York for its anonymity. He wanted to become invisible, his childhood wish. The argument with Catherine had discharged so many violent emotions that M had trouble remembering who he was. If he was no longer married then who was he?

He removed his wedding band and laid it on the dresser. Then he thought better of that and placed it in his billfold. He looked down at his bare hands, and wrists. The ring had left an indentation on his finger. He placed the thumb and forefinger of his right hand in the ring groove and traced the circle of bruised flesh.

Exiting the hotel, M turned south and walked alongside Central Park in the shade of the large overhanging hardwoods. It was early spring. Crocus and daffodils were in bloom, and flowering crab trees.

At 70th Street he looked across Fifth Avenue at a tall black gate which guarded – what? He couldn't remember. He hadn't been to the city in years. Crossing the street, he joined a small group of people waiting to enter the building.

It was an art museum. The handsome building had been a private residence that now housed a remarkable collection of Old Masters. There was an intimacy to the collection that seemed to invite M directly in. To look, undisturbed.

He wandered through the library and the family room and paused to admire an elegant staircase leading to the family's living quarters on the second floor of the residence, which was roped off. Standing at the base of the staircase next to the bust of a woman mounted on a pedestal, M looked at the forbidden second floor. A painting was hung on the landing, and two candelabras framed magnificent gold inlaid ornamentation that resembled the cabinets of a cathedral pipe organ.

M walked down the long dim hallway, stopping to look at a small painting. It was a Vermeer. A young girl sits at a dark table. Sheet music lies on the table, and a man holds with his thumb another sheet of music, which the girl also holds with both hands. But she is not looking at the man, whom M supposes is her teacher. Her face is turned toward the viewer, as if she had been interrupted at her music by M himself. She wears a look of mild astonishment. Her fine head, sheathed in a white head scarf, is turned away from her music. She looks directly at M.

Unnerved, M peered at the title of the painting: Girl, Interrupted at Her Music.

Two weeks after 9/11 M had traveled with Catherine to New York, where they bought a grand piano at Steinway Hall on West 57th Street. Catherine had been a music major in college, and taught private lessons for many years. Over time she had stopped giving recitals, and eventually she ceased to play. Her Baldwin spinet piano held dozens of family photos, of their children and their dogs and horses, but no music. Making a present of the Steinway, it was thought, would spur her to play again. And she did, for a time. But then the grand piano stood idle as well. No pictures were mounted on it.

Now as he returns the gaze of the girl in the painting, M thinks of his wife, whom he had left standing in the hallway of

36

their house, she holding the mail, he reaching for his car keys. Her face was gray and drawn. A strange, lonesome pity enters his heart to think of her. He had never known Catherine in her girlhood, had not in more than a dozen years asked her a question about how it was with her in those days when she was a child, raised by a widower, who managed to see to it that she continued her piano lessons after her mother died. By the time they had met, in college, Catherine was an orphan. He stares now, at the girl interrupted at her music, and he feels his soul run away, the solid world dissolve to tears. He tries to look away but the girl looks at him, startled.

Echo Park

for Emily Mortimer

The film industry began here southeast of Hollywood. The streets retain traces of the footsteps of Laurel and Hardy, Charlie Chaplin, the Three Stooges, and before that, a horse drawn streetcar trundled down the dirt road. Nicholson and Polanski shot Chinatown here. Later, Tom Waits would come, Michael Jackson shooting *Thriller*, sure. From your garden you can see a hummingbird and a coyote. At night the police helicopter circles overhead shining its powerful beam on real life criminals, though what's real in LA? A perpetual mystery. For six years you lived out of the same suitcase, filling it in London, pulling out an outfit a day for the acting jobs you started getting, finally. Such a strange place, so close to downtown where no one can be seen walking the empty streets. A cartographer might have mapped you on the edge of the known world, lit by the famous light, or cavorting in a Ridley Scott scene from *Blade Runner*, the glittering rain and shattered sound of a future world well lost. You escaped to the fog and damp of London when you felt you could not take another day. A city where one could take a walk, a city of parks. But no longer yours. You felt a stranger there, and then another audition, another job, Echo Park, suitcase. But in LA the seasons never change, the filmmakers' adoration of light never stops, the years go by and you were scared you would not be able to leave. People in LA live in denial of death, pretending the light, the wheatgrass, the pill, the new enema, the hairstylist's guru, the botoxed face – until the earth moves and you think, Bloody Hell, give me New York, a city on bedrock. But you stay in LA because it is possible to do nothing, and it is easy to avoid a hangover because no one wants to get drunk and besides you need to drive, even if it's just down the street So you're in bed early. You wake in the morning and can actually do things, can read and think, without feeling oppressed as in New York, by the Next Big Thing which must be done. But today someone recognized you at Il Cielo, a perfect stranger, and interviewers hang on your every word, or ask the same idiotic questions, and look at you, almost forty now, but still the raspy voice, now sexy, now squeaky, and there is nowhere to hide. As before the camera, then projected onscreen, nowhere to hide, nowhere to go, the room you've entered a dream of this room you now inhabit, for now every boy, every lost man teetering on the edge of a train that runs into the night through Echo Park and lays in your underwear drawer, the palms and the endless fiery plants and the layered levels of the nameless shining mountains, the important people and the filler people, and the parties that make you quiver like a bright paper streamer blown in the breeze, every last one of them will ask, "Must I follow her too?" Now is the time for you to go out into the light to congratulate whoever is left in our city, and look, I am totally taken with you, light a candle and place it here in my death wreath and let me blow you a crazy kiss. Oh, wow, I love you so much in so short a time, I'm yours, now what are you going to do with me? Why do I tell you these things, you are not even here.

I Love Sara L

I love Sara L. All day long I sit around and say to myself, I love Sara L. Sometimes I say it out loud for my approval. When I was in junior high school you would write the name of your girlfriend on your book covers. At the time I was in love with Rhonda Berryman from Waterbury Manor. Why did Waterbury Manor have all the cute girls? I don't know. New meaning to cluster fuck. Anyway, I love Sara L. I just love to say that. I love Sara L, I love Sara L. I never get tired of saying I love Sara L. No one ever called Rhonda, Rhonda, she was always Ronnie. She had reddish blonde hair, big hair, and blue eye shadow, and she looked kinda slutty, which was fine by me. I went to her house once. It was during that fifteen minute period when she was my girlfriend. I may have kissed her, I don't remember. If I didn't kiss her it's a shame but if I did kiss her it's a bigger shame in a way since you'd think a girl that slutty would at least kiss you in a way that you'd remember? Anyway, when I wrote Ronnie on my books boy did that get the looks! But that was her name, it was what she wanted to be called. No one would have known who Rhonda was. Mr. Cyr kidded me about it but he was an idiot. He stopped at my desk on his wanders around the room trying to find cheaters on the history test. He hovered with his old man breath above my desk looking concerned, in an assholian way. As an early adapter I had taken the practice of writing your girlfriend's name on your books to a new level, writing Ronnie on my skin. Specifically, all over my hands. Maybe Cyr thought I had the answers to the test written on my body but Ronnie wasn't an answer to anything. I don't know who got this tradition going of writing your girlfriend's name on books. It might have been Ossie Dahl but I doubt it. It might have been me, though I was never a starter. I was more an adapter. Someone would start something and I would adapt it if I liked it. Anyway, I love Sara L, I love Sara L, oh my god I love Sara L! I don't really remember what happened to Rhonda, I mean, Ronnie Berryman but somehow I kept going in the seventh grade and wound up as Vicki Morgan's boyfriend. *Incense and Peppermint* was a popular song at the time. No one knew what it meant but we had elaborate theories. A number one hit by Strawberry Alarm Clock. We didn't know what that meant either. The sixties went slower in Westchester than down in the city. Vicki had transferred in from Catholic school and was ready to cut it loose! I became her boyfriend by note. I could always write. In this note passed in history class I asked Vicki would she be my girlfriend? I ran the risk of having Cyr intercept the note but maybe I thought he would be relieved. Anyway, Vicki said yes! Not by return note. She just opened her formerly Catholic mouth and made an O with her lipsticked mouth. She had just come into lipstick from her lipstickless Catholic life at Saint Columbanus. She also had black fishnet stockings and blue eye shadow, which she may have gotten from Ronnie Berryman. They both lived in Waterbury Manor. What was it about that place? Anyway, I love Sara L, I love Sara L, I love Sara L. I say these words like a mantra. It gives me comfort, somehow. Vicki didn't stay my girlfriend for very long. Maybe I spelled something wrong in the note? Anyway, we stayed friends. But it really doesn't matter now does it because *I am* no longer in seventh grade and I love Sara L, I love Sara L, I *love* Sara L, I love Sara L.

    I love Sara L

    I love Sara L

    I love Sara L

    I love Sara L

    I love Sara L

I love Sara L
I love Sara L
I love Sara L
I love Sara L
I love Sara L
I love Sara L
I love Sara L
I love Sara L
I love Sara L
I love Sara L

I am so goddamn happy.

Announcement

Tom Hinson wakes up thinking of Scarlett Johansson. He yawns, throws back the covers, then steps sleepily into the shower. Kim has already left for work. He glances at the clock. He has a conference call in twenty minutes.

What is it about Scarlett Johansson. He gives this to himself as a project for thought. She is not the world's finest actor. But she has a quality Tom would like to name. He wants this for the day, more than his conference call, more than the security of his job, more than his failing marriage. He wants to know what it is that she has.

Two weeks ago Kim turned to him in bed and made an announcement. She was not an announcement person. In their eighteen year marriage announcements were few. They stuck to the corners, low-keyed everything. But Kim had been to a horse show, had ridden for the first time in years, had polished her saddles. Lying back in bed in jodhpurs, her hair pulled back, resting against the headboard, she looked radiant. She said look, I think I'm done, OK? I'm sorry.

Tom offered no resistance. It was clearly what she wanted. She had the reins. Neither of them knew what came next, but as they talked they began to believe that they would figure it out. Meantime, was there any essential reason not to continue on in the same house? They could not name one. What about separate rooms? Well, no. Not necessary. But it was a big house, if they wanted to. Sex? Was not out of the question. Tom thought, but didn't mention, that it seemed pretty much like the old arrangement.

He keeps the water cool against his skin, soaping his feet and his calves. He pauses over his belly, which is flattening. He has not been eating much. Work is a problem. Tom believes he will need a new job. Is this what is coming, the upheaval of everything? A planned destruction, like a building dynamited.

Water streams from his hair. It is her steadiness, Tom decides. Her directness. Her capacity to convey emotion through the smallest unforced gesture. He had watched Scarlett from her earliest work, the Redford movie. Bob had always been good with young actors. They had known each other in the early Sundance years, when Tom had made a small film. A passing acquaintance, a lifetime ago. Redford wouldn't remember. Tom no longer had an agent.

But Scarlett, he thinks. She has the ability to completely inhabit her body. Her sexiness stemmed from her confidence. She lived *though* her body, it was not her container, it *was* her, her way of expressing herself in the world. She had it at fourteen. Do most women understand this? He didn't know. Did women know their bodies better than men?

He and Kim were communicating better now. This surprised him. He wondered if there would be new relationships for each of them, and if it were possible, with a new love, to begin the relationship at the end, to treat each other with the honesty that seemed to arrive only now, when they were parting.

Tom Hinson steps from the shower into his bathrobe. He draws the terry cloth belt tight against his damp skin. Running his fingers through his hair, he finds a brush and combs it into place. He doesn't like how that looks, so he musses his hair and starts over. He picks up his razor and puts it down. He places it back in his shaving kit. He imagines Scarlett beside him, standing at the sink. She soaks his skin with a wet washcloth. She takes the can of shaving lotion and sprays a generous amount in her hand. She lathers his face with it, fingering the white cream just below his sideburns, then spreading out her pretty hand and swiping it all over his cheeks. Scarlett takes the can and refills her hand with cream, and whitens the strip where he once had a small moustache. Her soft hand passes along his jawline, then dabs at his chin, and under his neck. Till he looks like a mummy.

The phone rings. It's Kim.

"I didn't think I'd get you. Don't you have a conference call?" she says.

He takes the shaving cream can in his free hand and sprays the cream all over his right cheek. "In ten minutes," he says. He shifts the phone to his right hand and sprays his other cheek.

"What are you doing?" Kim asks.

"I'm shaving." He has piled the cream on so it sits high on his face.

Kim sighs. "I'm having a terrible day. Munger is on me again about the fucking report that was due last week, the report I put off doing because *he* hadn't got me the clearance I needed. The moron. Jesus." A silence ensues. "Tom, are you there?"

Tom has opened his straight razor and is delicately moving it down his face. He glances at his face in the mirror. He looks like a clown. The earpiece of the black phone is dipped in white foam. Flesh−colored stripes have appeared on his face from where he has passed the razor. He places the razor blade against his throat. If he pressed in, with how much pressure? He could add red to the black and white. All the pretty colors.

"Tom, are you OK? I'm worried. Are you going to be OK today? It's been two weeks, today."

"I'm fine," Tom says. He passes the blade between his lower lip and the knob of his chin. "I was thinking, what is it about Scarlett Johansson?"

"Just a minute," Kim says. Tom hears her talking to her secretary. He finds Kim's mascara in its pretty pink case, and traces a black line on the inside of his wrist.

"Sorry about that. What were we saying?"

"Scarlett Johansson."

"She knows what she wants," Kim says. "She moves like she believes it. She's what we would build if we could build people."

Tom considers this. Then asks, "Would you kiss her?"

He finishes shaving and presses a hot washcloth to his face, where he has nicked his chin. He tears off an inch of toilet paper and places it on the fresh cut.

"Of course," Kim had said.

That's Grace, Too

My son lies on the sofa bed in the living room with a red and yellow sleeping bag pulled up to his chin. The same bag, it's true, that I used to cover Kathleen the night we slept in the tent in Vermont. Rain falls faintly on the tin roof above our heads.

I like that this blanket that once covered Kathleen now covers him.

Rain fell that night in Vermont. We drove around the campground looking for the slot we'd rented. joking that two college graduates should be able to count. We had rented lot 45 but couldn't find it in the dark. Laughter was a relief. I started in on the tent while Kathleen pumped up the air mattresses. She looked over at me. I was having a harder time. The tent was new, it was dark by now, the instructions were useless, and it was coming slowly. I didn't want to ask our new neighbors for help. Or worse, her. When I got the tent up she looked pleased. We kissed in the light rain, then went inside to our new home.

We made love that night, safe and dry and happy. It rained all night. We had travelled a long way to arrive completely in that moment. I swear it, I was happy.

We didn't bother to zip the sleeping bag. It covered us both like a blanket, but as we slept she got most of it, and I shivered beside her, glad to give it to her, happy that this was something I could do for her. It pleased me that I could keep her warm, even if it was only for this one night.

One of the tent poles collapsed. It waved like a dog leg in the wind and the rain in the chilled night air. Kathleen got up to pee. She tapped the broken pole with her fingernail. I wondered if the tent would collapse. We shrugged and went back inside.

My son talks to me about a book set in Montreal, but I am thinking of the first meal I bought Kathleen, the little café where we kissed for the first time, admitted we were scared, and tried to see the future.

My son remarks how comfortable it is, this sleeping bag, and this pleases me. It pleases me that the bag that warms him once warmed Kathleen, even if it didn't warm me. The night that Kathleen and I used it (she more than me) I stayed up most of the night watching her. I combed my fingers through her hair, placing the long ends in my mouth. I smelled the smoky woods, heard the fire hiss as I stroked her arms, kissed her fingers, admired the swell of her breasts through her cotton shirt. We were lovers. And something else, we were friends

Later, we exchanged the tent for a motel room by the interstate. I'd lie in bed and listen to her shower, then ask if I could watch her do her makeup and hair. She'd brush it one hundred strokes, humming softly, standing absently in front of the mirror, planning her day. It was summer. I'd made this time for us, and we were happy. An interlude, she called it – she was giving me this *interlude*, giving it to us, and it was clear from the way she said it that it was full of grace, this moment. I tried to take it in, the way you look at the mountains when you're from the flats, not knowing when you'd get out west again, if maybe this was your last sight – how could you know? This is the way I looked at her at first light. I tried to memorize the way that she moved in that early morning motel light.

Things change, don't they? Some things you give up. If you're lucky you get more. And the *more* never replaces what you once had, it just stands tenderly beside it, guarding it maybe – or maybe it just makes it easier, I don't know. A new sight comes along, new memories, new ways of seeing. New people enter your life to move you on. No, the things you give up you don't ever get back, but if you're lucky you get new things, not replacements, exactly, but just new things to keep you moving. To keep you whole. And that's grace, too.

The Dress

It may have been the crown of Positano shot with sunlight, the descent to dinner at Black's on the beach, the road to Amalfi cutting back and forth in deep, blind turns, or the three bottles of red wine with people I barely knew. But on the long walk back up the hill, passing yet another boutique, just above the church, I say: "I no longer have anyone to buy a dress for."

Three women in our group respond with groans and offers. Later, I fall asleep to the poetry of failure.

The next day I go in search of a dress.

It takes a week to find one whose color reminds me of the streaked Italian sky. I find some black fuck—me heels in Roma, and settle in for the long flight home. The heels are out of the box, and I smile to think of some guy in customs going through my luggage and finding size five heels wrapped neatly in tissue paper next to my spent boxers.

The Positano woman who sold me the dress smiled and nodded at my choice. Dresses I'd picked over were strewn all over the small shop. The ones I liked best I had laid side by side, passing the fabric between thumb and forefinger. She placed the dress into a clear plastic bag and smiled. Prego. You want for wife? No, I said. But I thought of her runner's body, her baby—skinned bubble ass, nipples dark as raspberries on her small chest, those tiny feet coiled like steel springs as she ran from what troubled her. I knew she was not running toward me. But the dress, I imagined, would hang perfectly.

Two days later I hand off the dress in the lobby of her building, the heels too. I shush her cries of delight by drawing her deep into a hug, she sweating through a gray T-shirt from her run, me holding a taxi that will take me back to LaGuardia.

The next month I'm in Tribeca. Another hotel, another literary event. I thread onyx studs through the narrow slits of my tuxedo shirt, brush my hair, run a white cloth over patent leather shoes. Hotel life is blank, repetitive, and desultory, with the bareness of new furniture. The hall is deserted. I keep the shades drawn. The floor is scraped and varnished. I look at her picture in my phone and text to see when she will be ready.

I walk west on Duane Street, cut over to Chambers, walk down North End and there she is, long brown hair in wavelets against a coat of winter white. Underneath, I know, is the dress. She reaches up to hug me and gives me her whisky whisper: I need you to tie my dress. She takes my arm and walks unsteadily beside me. Try not to think of an elephant, I used to tell my classes. I try not to guess at the number of pills this time. But we walk arm and arm with dress untied.

Later, in Brooklyn, I remove her coat and knot a pretty silk bow against her shoulder blades. Inspect her narrow back. Adjust the flesh toned bra straps. Her white coat draped on my black tuxedoed arm, we enter the party. Where we drink fast to catch up, but then hurry to leave. Sharing a cigarette on a bench outside, she pulls me into a long smoky kiss, the shock of her tongue wet against my lips, then pushing against my teeth. Still kissing, she raises one leg and places it in my lap. A faint cracking, as of joints, shivering. I finger the black bow on her shoe. Her calves are muscled and tanned and smooth as glass. I once saw them curl into the fetal position as she sobbed into her pillow, then smashed her little fists into her mattress. Her fingernails bloodied and bitten to the quick. I would like to kiss her behind the knees. But instead we walk to the Bergen Street station, passing storefronts where we see our reflection in the chilly pane. Bells from a church fill the air. We ride in silence back to the island of Manhattan. Where she quietly takes my hand and kisses my fingers. We pass the speeding headlight of another train and her white throat appears. I hear again that little girl voice when she finds two small cuts I hadn't known were there. Maybe I smashed them against the elevator door at the party thinking of her ex, or maybe I bruise more easily these days, but the blood is dull red, and she says, Baby, you're cut. And then we are at the hotel and I realize it will be her.

Therapy

You go, "OK, OK. So, let's say that I am Miranda, and I go ..."

I forgot what you said next because that was *so* inappropriate.

We're not gonna have an affair, but we cross more lines in a week than the Dallas Cowboys.

An hour later I'm at dinner with Miranda and she blurts out, "I want to fuck Don Draper from *Mad Men*."

I spit my cabernet.

How can you not love women like this?

So then my wife goes, "What, don't *you* want to fuck Betty Draper?" She arches the eyebrow.

"Miranda, please. I don't fuck Republicans."

"Well, that never stopped you before."

Zing.

I thought about saying, "You cannot prove that," but resisted, which is why this divorce patter works so well.

It's those tiny accommodations.

So I go, "Well, not knowingly."

And she spits her cabernet.

Scripts

Beat Sheet

Mother is late again. She pulls up and Zach throws himself on the floor. She's promised a treat if he behaves at the beach. He has Bobby's soft Augusta drawl. "Ass cream, Gramma, ass cream."

We stop to give Jenna a lift to the airport. She knows how mother feels about her work. So on the drive over to her apartment she texts me, "Contract girl 4 for Vivid=No anal and guys wear condoms." Jenna is five one and sculpted. Guys in high school creamed when they saw her.

Mother drives while Jenna sits beside me and continues to text. "New name Savannah Haze. My brand re−launch." Zach reaches his dimpled arms, and Jenna / Savannah gives him a big kiss on his neck. He giggles and that does it, she's giving him busters now, loving all over his little neck.

Jenna tried to get me to go with her to the audition but Bobby got shipped to Afghanistan in the surge. We could use the money. Mom wants to help but Bobby has his pride. I have no earthly skills. Jenna does girl girl but she never made a pass at me. I kid her about it and act offended. One of the Vivid contract girls fell in love and refused boy girl for a long time. Word got out and she lost lots of money. She's back to anal and feet now, Jenna says.

We drop Jenna curbside. She has just enough time for her flight to LAX. I get out and walk her inside. Zach keeps screaming for ass cream. Mom says don't be long, dear. She has a long frown for Jenna.

Jenna pulls me into a hug and tells me Bobby will be OK, she swears. She'll say a novena. It must be all over my face. She asks me to water her plants while she's gone. She's away a month at a time. She bought a new condo in Studio City when her agent got her the Vivid gig. She's relieved. She says she has sex less than me now, her contract is that good. I tell her I'm happy for her but no one has sex less than me. I miss Bobby awful. Jenna tells me I can jill off to her movies, she'll send me some. I tell her no thanks. She has new peep toe shoes. Her toes look like ruby candy. She's my friend since second grade.

At the beach an old man watches from his balcony. He's got binoculars. I tug at my top, then flip him off and run after Zach, who is barking. He thinks he's a dog.

A Treatment

The Director watches from the balcony of his high room, tracking the women and their little boy as they make their way to the island beach near Savannah. The mother is fair, pixie cut, the daughter tan, free of affect, connected and purposeful.

10 a.m. The sun scorches. The Director says that we are too afraid of death to love wisely or to discover beauty; forfeiting beauty in exchange for love we begin to die before we have learned to live.

To cast and crew he says what torture it is to play opposite an actor who looks at you and sees someone else. He grabs the actress, the actor: *if everything around me were true how would I behave?*

The Director lifts his binoculars. A man walks past the two women, who struggle with the toddler's seat buckle. The girl is quick.

The Director sits in a raised chair at the pool. Below, on the beach, the women pull the boy in his red wagon. The mother shakes her head, rolls her high shoulders, cracks her long neck. The girl is twenty-two, too old for the part. Elise, his producer, texted him that his lead is back in rehab. Her boyfriend too.

Every action has a purpose. The beach girl bends at the waist to help her son with his pail and shovel. She is within reach of her little boy, available to him, a terrible beauty promising connection but remaining essentially unavailable. Nothing we do is neutral. The Director believes that only what happens before the age of eighteen is essential, he wants to be that buried child. Girl as Mom. As actress. Every actor's life is broken in half trying to escape self-awareness. At the moment you lose it you diminish your receptivity to experience. The best actors learn to hide as creative life becomes a shield, a way of keeping life at a distance. It saddens him. The girl is ruined, he thinks, even while embracing her beautiful distortions.

Better to watch her bury her boy in sand. Buried child. His delighted squeals, the easy grace of the grandmother's smile. A day at the beach, and nothing more.

Certain tribes of aboriginal descent believe that a photograph can steal a soul, imprisoning it within its amalgam of polyester, celluloid, salts and gelatin. The Director smiles to think himself a thief of souls. He leaves the Pentax camera around his neck. The girl will go untouched, unnoticed, unremarked, the perfect line of her body undisturbed. A role must have continuous being and unbroken line. He watches her, preserving all necessary distance, until at last he raises his weary arm and makes the sign of the cross over her, over the mother and the boy, and the beach, as if in a papal blessing, as if his heart is not rent.

Shooting Scripts

She has two dimples just above her perfect ass, dimples you have seen before in a woman you once knew in a life long ago. You order a chair and umbrella to be placed alongside her encampment: a large pile (monogrammed Louis Vuitton waterproof canvas bags, cooler, red wagon heavily laden), and you wait. Waiting is what you do best

The young woman, when she approaches, looks like Kate Moss at twenty—three. Tousled blonde hair below her shoulder blades. Four inch silver teardrop earring, left side, closest to you. Her mother lovely as well, her hair in a blunt cut, a one—piece swim suit. The little boy is delightful, curly blond hair, uncut, a boy of two. For him they pull the big red wagon on the beach. They arrange their lives around him. They follow his every move, the male of the species. He carries pail and shovel in his starfish hands. Women without men, at the beach.

But the girl is twenty—three — can still be called a girl, before the sadness of twenty—four, or worse, twenty—nine, before the requisite changes of twenty—five, when the world calls women like her to account, to questions she does not now entertain, the girl at twenty—three, she stops your heart.

You have known her, you know her now. You smile at the mother and go on watching behind your summer hat of straw, your large striped beach glass. Under the ocean — blue umbrella in the summer sun.

The girl wears a black string bikini and as she watches her boy, places both hands on her hips.

The little boy has a sturdy body. He digs his shovel into the wet sand, then abandons his toys to chase a dog into the soupy surf. Both women run after him. You lift your fork to your mouth, then stop, exhausted. Eating seems like such work, is there no end to eating, must we go on doing this simple act forever? The girl bends at the waist to help her boy. Her breasts do not separate nor do they hang. Her line is perfect.

Her chest is small, her thighs and legs, everything well–proportioned, but her ass and hips are kept from being too small, she has escaped looking depleted only by giving birth to that boy.

Her child has run off again. He kicks a ball under your chair. Now she moves toward you, smiles.

"I'm sorry," she says.

She is sorry. A lifetime of apologies. They simply can't, and never do, apologize enough. Beauty and her shade, sorrow. Her mother looks and smiles too. We go on smiling. You lift your weary arm.

When they go you'll keep coming back for her. You will wait. A week, a month, she may be nowhere in sight, yet present, still. Each day you will see her more clearly. She has made every person on earth seem unnecessary.

Stab at It

On the summer lawn of the hospital we walk toward each other. Another emergency night. I read somewhere that the Tower of London employed its own full–time executioner. Do you remember that night you kicked your dying cigarette into a thin patch of grass outside a bar in the East Village? You stubbed the cigarette with the toe of your new black boot and watered it with beer from your mug. When Mord the executioner did his job a comet littered the London sky with sparks of terror. I found your hairbrush in my top dresser drawer. Strands of your hair wove around metal prongs like Medusa's snakes. Now summer is ending. In the distant woods the smoke of many small cook fires. I expected this from everyone else. But not from me. You were a girl with her head caught in the bars of the banister. It wasn't easy to stay in the present. I have urges to move backward, to grasp at silhouettes that are no longer. The grass is wet and heavy with morning. We walk toward each other on the blue lawn. Pull two chairs out of the sun and into the spreading shade of the cigarette tree.

Gaspar

Shattered sounds of summer storms. North of us, the bark of distant dogs. Trees crashed around us but Gaspar went on speaking. I could no longer help him. He spoke in circles, of the sea giving up its dead and water receding. His voice was liquid and his skin, paper. He was still in his ruined tux. I had chased him this far from the museum. We were not far from the petting zoo. The great park was empty for once. The day had lost its warmth. Gaspar fed a cigarette into his tired mouth and signaled for a light. I lit him. Do you know, he asked, what it is to be intimate? I had to admit I didn't. Sitting downwind, I coughed a dry cough. He grimaced and stamped his foot. It is when you feel safe with someone who carries the fire, he said. Someone who will never betray you, or force you to act in any way unlike yourself. There are certain men whose collapse is hidden. He tossed his cigarette into a puff of new air. The sky went orange, and then pink while I waited. Those who love us are those who rehearse nothing. When we meet it feels like an accident but the lines are ready, everything is in place. He described her nakedness, dresses hanging in a closet, late dinners, her whiskey voice on the phone. All of these things weigh something, he said. You know their weight in the instant they are gone. He was a wound I wanted to touch.

April 9

She steps into the empty restaurant where I am seated at the bar and gives me her half hug, smiling in my arms but still moving in that New York way, in street motion, orbiting invisible planets, moon and stars, a complete system of desire. Her black coat and boots match my black sweater. She's in town for another woman, but the other woman hasn't shown so there we are, talking of children, of literature and art and husbands, daughters, wives, the schedules of surgeons. At a table our waiter cannot wedge a word. You two like another drink — yes! — to order now? No, fucking Christ! No lull, only the steady beat of people who'd escaped the blankness of the blank screens, thrilled for the company of strangers. Finally, the impatient bartender dims the restaurant lights. We drop four twenties and spill onto 29th Street, walking east. Spring. In the chilled air we hail a yellow cab and I see her to it and the words stop. That night in the Waldorf mirror I am asking what was that? Asleep alone in the big bed I wake at 4 am and think that only a few things have happened to me in my life but some of them I have felt deeply.

Just Here

I moved out as green leaves darkened on the twisted trees. She slept in her pajamas on the sofa. I placed the keys on the kitchen counter and pulled the door closed. The snows have not come but left behind are the sounds of summer in my old neighborhood. No children's laughter splashes from an open hydrant; no small bark from a frightened dog. No purple woods appeared beyond the railroad tracks at my new house. No girls tanned and wet from the reservoir walk by my front door or wave as I sit alone on the stoop. Only the leaves, dropping. And everything that was just here again was gone

Funeral

Patrick Quinn fingers his collar and watches the funeral director instruct the pallbearers. The grave site is steep. Two days ago the widow had joked with him, Father, you'd better wear your golf shoes with cleats.

Quinn follows six beefy pallbearers to the rear of the hearse where the funeral director, a woman, gives directions. She is dressed in a smart black pants suit, contoured at the waist and hips, three quarter sleeves, high—waisted pants with flared leg openings, and sensible black pumps. The pallbearers look like high school linebackers. They can't take their eyes off her, either.

Quinn has worked with her before, but where? His parish draws folk from three rural counties, cradle to grave Episcopalians who line up for death and are plucked monthly from the back rows of the country church where he has served for twelve years.

A small plane drones overhead, and a late summer breeze blows through oak and maple trees. Below, a creek flows steadily to the Little Miami, from there to the Ohio River, and eventually into the Mississippi. Reared in New Orleans, Quinn has never gotten used to the staid funerals of these stoic Midwesterners.

Veronica left him for a podiatrist in town. In bed watching a new vampire series, she'd turned to him and said, "Jesus, Quinn, I thought you knew? We weren't exactly discreet." But Quinn hadn't known. In the parish, he is always the last to know. People hide bad news. Quinn has booked a flight to Connemara,

County Galway. But first, this funeral. This woman director. What is her name?

He opens the Book of Worship and recites the opening sentences. The psalms and the prayers he intones solemnly, in plain song, as the widow had requested. Quinn is conscious of his brittle tenor, and of the woman who stands beside him, watching.

Frankie. Her name is Frankie. They had ridden out to St. Paris in the black hearse for the Bleeker funeral, not long after Veronica moved out, a week before their twentieth anniversary. Which he will spend in Ireland, alone.

Quinn listens to Frankie's voice rise beside him, a low alto. She uses the old language, forgive us our trespasses, as we forgive those who trespass against us. Placing his right hand on the casket, above the silent head, he stands on the narrow spit of land between the casket and Frankie's small feet, on green Astroturf that covers freshly dug earth.

Quinn pronounces the benediction. He plucks a white rose from the spray on the casket and gives it to the widow, who breaks into tears. Quinn comforts her with the ancient wisdom of the church, aware that Frankie has not left his side. His parish is comprised of mostly post—menopausal women, and Quinn feels the heat from Frankie's body, not two feet away. He recalls that her boyfriend is a body builder, a hypochondriac unable to sire a child. She is the lapsed daughter of a deceased fundamentalist minister in town, a man Quinn despised for his narrow—mindedness.

Birds sing their late summer song. The creek moves fast, the current deep. An orange kayak floats downstream. Quinn has parked his BMW in the shade of a live oak. He bought the car after the divorce, a gift to himself.

The family scatters. Happy to be done with the funeral, Quinn thinks of his upcoming trip to Connemara. Frankie trades war stories with two cemetery caretakers, men Quinn has worked with often. Quinn laughs at their recycled stories. He would like to take the BMW's top down and follow the creek around the cemetery.

Frankie recalls a picture-taking ceremony. Family members took turns leaning into the casket with their faces next to the corpse, she says. They had big cheesy grins. They handed me a camera and made me snap away, till everyone had a keepsake. I'm sure it all wound up on Facebook.

She has braces, the kind that blend in with the teeth, so all you see is a thin white wire. On the drive to the cemetery she'd confessed to Quinn that she was often accused of being too perky for funerals. She bares her right arm and shows them her new tattoo, a grocery list: bread, milk, cheese, eggs, pizza, beer. Quinn laughs. He tells her it would look even better if she'd crossed off a few items.

They admire the day, the gentle breeze, the dexterity of the kayaker. Quinn says it's a great day to take a ride in a convertible, and hears a trio of voices. "What convertible?"

Mine, Quinn says. Oh, you didn't, Frankie says.

You got a minute? I can show you how it works. Frankie shrugs and says sure. The men walk back to their truck.

Quinn waves the key like a wand at the keyless ignition and fires the 300-horsepower twin-turbo engine. The BMW is fire engine red with a cream interior. The dual exhaust pipes play a throaty duet. Frankie arches a trained eyebrow. She has a small cluster of freckles around her nose, and that one clear line across her teeth.

Quinn presses a button and the red top begins to lift. The top slides back into the trunk. Four windows disappear.

Sweet, Frankie says. She opens the passenger side door.

Quinn punches up the volume of *Thunder Road*, and navigates the creek bend. He slows to a stop to allow a family of ducks to cross. Frankie's alto harmonizes with Springsteen, "the door is open but the ride ain't free." The goslings follow their mother in a straight line.

Quinn sets his clerical collar on the console. In one week summer will be over, and it will be Labor Day. Frankie is no more than thirty. All men are mortal, he remembers from logic class. Socrates is a man, therefore Socrates is mortal.

Frankie twirls Quinn's clerical collar like a Frisbee. The ducks make their duck noises, and the creek flows. Quinn lifts the collar from Frankie's pretty finger and places it around her slender neck. He prays every prayer he knows.

Giacometti

Giacometti reclines on the couch. He smokes my last cigarette and points to an object behind me, a spare structure of thin uprights and horizontal beams in which there is something like a flying bird, the backbone of an animal, a female figure, and a hollowed out spatulate shape with a ball in front of it. He tells me that only a few things had happened in his life but some of them he had felt deeply.

"I don't know by what terms my father came to terms with his grief," he says. "His sadness was of the kind that is patient but without hope."

My girlfriend enters the room. She crosses herself and kisses me shyly on the cheek. Then sits at Giacometti's feet. His shoes are caked with mud. She plays absently with the mud, scraping it from his shoes with her long unpainted fingernail. Giacometti ignores her, and keeps speaking.

"The artist conserves a splinter of ice in the heart," he says. "After I left my village of Borgonova in Switzerland, I was always a tourist, wherever I was."

Giacometti reaches down to play with Maura's hair. In a corner of the dark room stands a statue of Maura. Her body is elongated, thin as a nail and as big as a cigarette pack. When Maura has asked why he had done this he had said nothing, but shrugged his slender shoulders. To me, later, he had said, "When I look at a woman the longer I look the thinner they become. I work by paring away what is not essential, work until one touch more and things vanish. But do you love her, this Catholic girl?"

I nodded my head, yes. "Very much," I said.

Giacometti sighed. "I have no thoughts on this," he said. "All my thoughts are in the clay."

It was spring break in Cambridge. We had traveled two days and two nights to be with him in his studio. There were letters of introduction, which he ripped up and burned in his furnace. Yet when he had answered the door he acted as though he knew us and had been expecting us for some time. Later he told us it was as if we had always been there.

"The artist must be taken in by his own tricks," Giacometti says. "He must begin by pleasing himself. This is essential. His mouth must be the first that drops open in surprise."

When he says this Maura reaches out her mud–streaked fingers and caresses his cheek. She throws open the wide window. In the gloaming, a yawning face appears in the clouds. The sky is painted with a bruised lead and sepia tone that will afterwards haunt me, as too this room, with its objects alive and dead at the same time.

Maura is in his lap. She kisses his thin lips, her hand on his cheek, but he makes no acknowledgement of her urgent Irish kisses. He only takes her hand and wipes away the mud.

Now even the farthest windows have gone dark. And it appears that the dark needs us, wants us for itself. We want to lie with Giacometti in his unmade bed on the floor in his studio.

The week before he died I confessed to Maura that I didn't think I could stand it without him. And she said to me, "I've lived with death my whole life. And I know that the people we love we carry with us, always. They are part of us."

Why I Write Such Good Songs, Coyote

We got the job by lies and defended our honor by night on the Hill in Saint Louis. Jimmy was thirty and I was forty and we'd met in the state pen. The foundry was hot and shitty but the pay was good and the corner bar cashed your paycheck no questions asked.

The day we got the axe we handed our severance over to Annette and settled in. Annette was from the Illinois side. East Saint Louis but bled Cardinal red. She had two female cousins in town. Toward midnight they showed up and we knew we were in trouble. They heard us thinking and slid their stools closer. The blonde had a ragged way of breathing that sounded like there was a chain saw buzzing in her chest. Her friend had a hawk nose and the long–waisted look that Jimmy fancied. There was one purse between them as they said they shared everything. They started out as threes but we drank them up to sevens and then eights.

We both had wives who'd gone on to other men while we were in the pen which of course held only men. Women made me jump and I mean any woman. That extra hole made a difference.

Since the blonde was mine I tried the Heimlich demonstration which I figured was both edgy and educational. Plus I wanted to hear that chest rattle. She sounded like a box of cough drops being shaken. After I saved her several times Jimmy tried out his pretty good coyote call which hawk nose captured on her cell phone camera. Then we started Tequila shots.

I inspected the women and gauged our chances. The blonde was called Roxy and the other was Michelle. Roxy rattled nearby. I knew if she was primed up she'd probably fuck a rock pile if she thought there was a snake in it. Then again, a hard dick has no conscience. If you live on the railroad tracks the train's going to hit you, Grandpa used to say. We hadn't been sober in a week. Hangover thoughts are real long thoughts.

We drank past closing time and then some. Jimmy got the idea to go to his ex's house. He formed a belief that she was out of town visiting her mother in Cape Girardeau. Annette informed us that we had to go somewhere and this elevated Jimmy's belief into one worth entertaining. What was astonishing was that the women thought so too. Which sort of endeared them to me.

Roxy drove her '78 Ford 150 pickup and I rode shotgun. She played a Bee Gees cassette tape and rasped along on the chorus of *How Deep is Your Love*. Michelle and Jimmy were squeezed in beside us with Jimmy on the door and we crossed the Eads Bridge this way into East Saint Louis. The Mississippi was black wavy ink but the bridge held steady. Roxy drove with two stone cold hands. The pickup had one headlamp but it was a good one.

Jimmy had Michelle's shirt half off. Michelle had her hand on me but Roxy knocked it back off. We drove that way for a while. Hand tugging at zipper and hand smacked. Hand in waistband and hand smacked. Jimmy tried to help Michelle but got smacked too. I was hoping the house would show up soon but we were lost. We twisted around on some back roads and Jimmy called out the turns and worked Michelle's bra straps down. It was almost first light.

The house had burned down and all there was around the foundation were dry burdocks and chokecherries and one sugar plum the bears had broken down to get at the fruit. Meanwhile the women were on their stomachs on a mattress that'd been left and both of their bare bottoms were showing plain as day. There was an old upright piano in the foundation square. The big sky was getting lighter and if their butts were cameras it seemed like they were taking my picture.

An Indian story came to mind from out west. Every time a man would screw he'd bleed to death because women had sharp teeth in their articles. It wasn't until a coyote came along and pulled the teeth out that men could screw without dying and get the human race started. This is why the coyote is thought to be sacred.

Well OK but Jimmy's about as low down as a snake's dick. So he looks at these four women on the bed through his one good eye until he figures out that there's only two of them after all and only one for him. He asked the one if she'd mind getting up on the piano and could she lay out so he could sing to her. Michelle scrambled up with no problem and lay there leaning her head on a hand. He sang *Yes, we have no bananas* and she started laughing. It's what we sang to each other of a morning in the pen to keep our spirits up. I hoisted Michelle up on the piano beside her cousin. She looked right as rain. I stood partway up and she slid down. Her ass hit the keys in a nice way like the lost chord. We did it right there which wasn't easy.

Some Pianos

A woman I knew died decades ahead of her burial. We were
children when we met but only by a little; we helped raise each
other, bearing witness at last to the mystery of sex. She played
piano for hours in the moldy practice rooms of the dingy college
we attended on old upright pianos that have since been sent
shrieking to the junkyards of Ohio, their strings loosened and
bare ivory keys stripped, their skinny mahogany legs hacked to
pieces. And like children we watched each other warily at the
cemetery after the tornado that carefully placed the second floor
of our dormitory in the middle of the street. The first floor was
intact, and so were we, so I asked her to marry me. Which
seemed a good idea. That way we wouldn't be lonely and our
"sensitivity" would no longer go unnoticed and besides we
would one day have children, blond and good, with her blue
eyes and my whatever, that *je ne sais quoi* that I prized at the
time. We bought a grand piano at Steinway Hall on 57th Street
after 9/11, chased uptown by the dust of death and awakening
from dreams of miniature jumpers stuck in the icing of white
wedding cakes, hundreds of these cakes posted to bulletin boards
in Union Square. I kited a check and put the balance on a gold
Amex card and a week later the piano arrived. She never played
it.

Some mornings it is hard to shake the chill, though Ohio is
far from the peaked mountains of Colorado where we spent the
first years of marriage. And here by the railroad tracks the
summer sun burns away every imperfection and I hang like a
noose loosely attached to a mirror that shows the clear reflection

of her long disappointment, and await the night when there is nothing left to beg.

In Venice

They talked as evening fell. She'd appeared in the doorway at Harry's Bar in Venice, barelegged but in heels. It was her voice he remembered from their days in New York, scornful and warm above the shrieking subway.

The lights were blinking on in the buildings surrounding the piazza. She stared at a table of people, merry across the room and loud as Russians. Light gleamed from the polished wood of the bar. Lines of glasses stood as icy soldiers on the narrow shelves.

Something was missing in him. Women had always done anything to find out what it was. Across the room someone was saying, "When you've been married you want to be married again."

American college girls came into the bar drunk. A half hour later six girls in unison kicked their bare legs in the brilliant light, to scattered applause. They went on talking. She drank looking directly at him. Across the room the conversation continued. Americans. "Women fall in love when they get to know you," one of them said. "Men are just the opposite. When they finally know you they're ready to leave."

The bartender passed a dense icy glass to the man seated next to them. Summer was ending. Outside, the first winds of autumn ruffled the green water of the Grand Canal, wide as a river. A giant cruise ship was in port. Bilge water poured from its stern. He wished again that he was in love.

"In Barcelona," she was saying, "is a cathedral that was never completed. Built by Antonio Gaudi, an architect more like a saint." She filled her lungs with smoke from her cigarette. "He was hit by a streetcar walking to church. He lay in the street, bleeding. No one recognized him." He reached for her. She let herself be held, but she was like a huge dog, leaping from his arms. "The cathedral that was never built," she said. "It has doors that lead both ways into empty air."

They walked out of the bar. A wave of pigeons rose into the air before a trotting dog. The lights in some palazzos shone. He imagined, in the curtained upper floors, the long legs of countesses uncoiled, shaved and smooth, slithering on silk sheets. The sky became violet. Two men sat at a small table trimming artichokes. The blue cars of the *carabiniere*. Bags of rice and dry beans beside the table where the men continued their work. A girl with a tailored coat walked past them with a scarf wrapped around her head. He felt that his life was clarifying.

A taxi pulled up and she stepped inside, pulling him in behind her. The car rattled the narrow street. They took the A4 highway west. In Verona, the points of the tall steeples. Schoolgirls in dark skirts and blouses blindingly white. One stood off by herself. Her pale legs shook like small sticks. The woman made the taxi stop for the girl. That was me, she said to him. She whispered words to her in Italian. The girl sat beside them in the taxi. The window of the Mercedes glided up. It started to rain. His room was on the corner. A long dark corridor, heavy drapes of forest green and matching cushions on the white window sills. The towels a pale green with the name of the hotel in white.

The girl did not look at any of this. He knelt to remove her shoes. She peeled a strip of pink paper from a menu on the nightstand. Her fingernails were short and clear. In the morning there will be breakfast rolls and cappuccino. A sliced pear. Gleaming spoons on a starched white tablecloth. His life was simple. In the morning the air will be pure and cool.

One More Thing

The second thing Annie Riser did after receiving her diagnosis was to find a realtor in the Yellow Pages and put her house up for sale. It was a big house in the Connecticut suburbs with ugly casement windows that were difficult to clean, and Annie knew she wouldn't miss it. She understood that Ronald would disapprove.

The first thing she did was book a flight to Colorado. It was mid–winter, and the western sunshine surprised her. In Denver she rented an all–wheel drive vehicle and drove to Ouray. Her husband had died twenty years before, caught in a spectacular avalanche while skiing in the back country near Telluride and Annie had never been to Telluride or to Colorado. Annie chose Ouray for the big mineral springs pool, and for its proximity to the backcountry where Ronald, Sr. had met his death.

Now Annie stretches her body in the hottest section of the pool and watches the passing traffic, people who seem comically white. Steam rises from the hot water and hovers over the pool as over a tea cup, and to Annie, staring at her scissoring legs, it feels as if she is living in a cloud. But when she raises her head to see the spectacular red cliffs, and the mountains that ring the pool, bathed in late afternoon light, she sees a family of deer picking their way through the foot high snow just beyond the protective railing of the pool. The deer come at the same time each afternoon. Annie wonders where they go each night.

Her cell phone rings. Annie picks up the phone, to see who is calling, then lets it go to voicemail. Scrolling through the menu, she selects silent.

Annie lies in the water with her feet braced at the bottom of the pool and her arms behind her head. She pulls her upper body into a series of crunches. She doesn't feel sick. Neither had Rose at Stage 3, when both women had felt free to speak of hope. But Annie understands what is coming, what cannot be stopped. She understands also that it is the third thing she did after receiving her diagnosis that will set things in motion.

Annie is 72. She lost her youngest child three years ago to the same ravenous form of ovarian cancer. Rose struggled but succumbed at last upstairs in the rambling Connecticut house, in her girlhood bedroom. Divorced and childless, Rose had wanted to go home to her mother's house to die. Together they had made the hospice arrangements.

An enormous man enters the hot water section. His big belly overhangs his fashionable trunks. He wears a beige hat with ear flaps that reminds Annie of Lawrence of Arabia. The fat man nods at Annie and collapses into the hot water like a descending hippo, one leg at a time, his enormous head and pink nostrils disappearing into the mist.

Annie glances at her phone. It lights with a silent call. She sighs and places the cold screen to her wet ear.

"Mom, what the fuck! You put the house up for sale? Why didn't you talk to me? Where the hell are you, anyway?"

"Are you at the house now, Ronald?"

"Mom, you understand that I am a realtor, right? You do understand that, correct? What'd you do, pick this idiot out of the phone book? What were you thinking? He couldn't even get his sign into the ground straight. Where the hell *are* you, Mother?"

Annie snaps the phone off. The third thing she had done after getting her diagnosis was to call an auction service. She gave orders to set all her belongings on the snowy lawn of her house and to accept the highest bid. Proceeds will go to the Greenwich Ovarian Cancer Fund in Rose's name.

Annie looks at the dying light of Ouray, the last bit of sunshine on the highest peak, how many miles away? How cold would it get on that peak tonight, Annie wonders, in the harsh Colorado winter. How odd it was, to be warm in the cold, lying in the mineral springs pool. Contradictions. Like Rose, healthy and strong and dying, painlessly. Bit by bit our life slips away, Annie thinks. Better to go out strong than to fade molecule by poisoned molecule, to endure the body's cruel betrayal, or a son's callous disregard for his mother's wishes, his taunting of her politics, his criticism of hospice care, his mirthless rich life in a diseased community of the living.

The phone rings again. As compassionately as she can manage she explains things to her remaining child. Ronnie, she says, about tomorrow. One more thing, she says, and pauses. She lays it out, what is coming, what cannot be stopped.

Annie places the phone in her bag. Pulling herself up by the rails she steps out of the pool, her swim suit dripping water. Looking at the darkening mountains, she climbs over the protective railing. She places her bare feet carefully in the deer tracks. She walks out into the Colorado night.

Acknowledgments

A number of these stories appeared in slightly different form elsewhere, and in some cases titles and names of characters have been changed.

Grateful acknowledgment is made to the following magazines, where these stories were first published: *Wigleaf, Mississippi Review, U City Review, elimae, Word Riot, Necessary Fiction, Bluestem, Fogged Clarity, Short Story America, Metazen, Twelve Stories, Pure Slush, Fwriction, Doctor T.J. Eckleburg Review,* and *The Good Men Project.*

Other books from *Pure Slush*

For the complete catalogue of *Pure Slush*
anthologies and single author books,
print books and eBooks,
visit the *Pure Slush Store* at
http://pureslush.webs.com/store.htm

falling and other poems
by Gary Percesepe
ISBN: 978‑1‑925101‑24‑9
Originally published November 2013

Percesepe's poetry seems straightforward but
is as complex as flowers, as summer shade and
layers of snowfall, available to all but folded
around secrets only broken lovers or
philosophers grasp, and contained by no
borrowed forms but original truths and no
meter but the throbs of a heart. He here
assays breakfast making and love making and loss and memory and
time and husbands and wives and offspring and always, always, the
elegance of the line, the object plain or sublime or both, the landscapes
of sex, sorrow and high style.

James Robison

The Merrill Diaries
by Susan Tepper

ISBN: 978–0–9922778–2–6
Originally published July 2013

The Merrill Diaries follows a quirky young woman running from a couple of doozy marriages but mainly from herself. Humor as well as pathos are discovered as our narrator opens up to the world, takes risks, and learns. The language is whip smart, the characters live and breathe on the page   *Bonnie ZoBell*

The Merrill Diaries takes you on a wild ride ... This novel in stories is the end of innocence and the start of "the broken tracks, the roads where the river has flooded over."   *Gloria Mindock*

The language is spare and intense getting quickly into the staccato rhythms of Merrill's slap–dash life. Great fun, yet sad too.   *Gay Degani*

Hard
by Dusty–Anne Rhodes

ISBN: 978–1–291–37970–9
Originally published April 2013

Dusty–Anne Rhodes' non–fiction has earned praise for its honesty and quirky ability to see beneath the surface and bring out the human in its subjects.

Her vignettes explode and when they are done, our familiar furniture is not in the same place. For that matter, neither are we.   *Tim Page*

Her empathy for the emigrant, the downtrodden and the faceless, shines through in this gentle and deeply insightful book.   *JP Reese*

Glass Animals
by Stephen V. Ramey
ISBN: 978−1−300−66220−4
Originally published January 2013

Ramey takes on the richness of his characters' emotional and physical torment and delivers something morbidly fascinating and keen. A great first collection.   *Kristine Ong Muslim*

Equally irreverent and real, these forty−five flash and micro−sized tales left me feeling as though I'd spent time inside the heads of forty−five different people.
H.G. Estok

Wild: a collection
by Gill Hoffs
ISBN: 978−1−4717−4215−6
Originally published June 2012

Gill Hoffs' writing, fiction and non, swells with the power of life, sometimes life at the expense of other lives, but always animated and alive.   *Ronnie Scott*

Vestal Aversion
by Matt Potter
ISBN: 978−1−4717−1397−2
Originally published May 2012

His range is wide, exploring topics from extramarital affairs to mean−spirited childhood pranks, and his characters always come through as very human ... entertaining and often thought−provoking. *Richard Bon*

www.ingramcontent.com/pod-product-compliance
Lightning Source LLC
Chambersburg PA
CBHW030540180626
46810CB00005B/1943